Emma Thomson's
felicity Wishes®

Star Surprise

and other stories

Hodder
Children's
Books

A division of Hodder Headline Limited

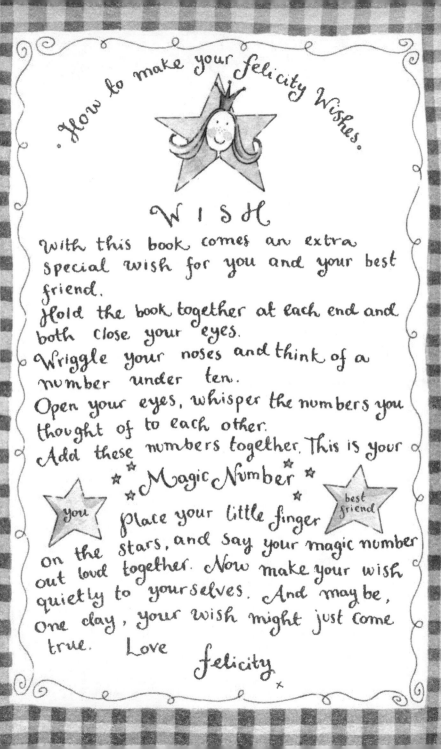

How to make your felicity Wishes.

WISH

With this book comes an extra special wish for you and your best friend.

Hold the book together at each end and both close your eyes.

Wriggle your noses and think of a number under ten.

Open your eyes, whisper the numbers you thought of to each other.

Add these numbers together. This is your ✶ Magic Number ✶

you

best friend

Place your little finger on the stars, and say your magic number out loud together. Now make your wish quietly to yourselves. And maybe, one day, your wish might just come true. Love

felicity

x

For lovely Lili India Rose, love Mummy x
E.V.T

FELICITY WISHES

Felicity Wishes © 2000 Emma Thomson
Licensed by White Lion Publishing

Text and Illustrations © 2004 Emma Thomson

First published in Great Britain in 2004 by Hodder Children's Books

A Catalogue record for this book is available from the British Library

ISBN 0 340 88241 7

Printed and bound in Great Britain by Bookmarque Ltd, Croydon, Surrey

The paper and board used in this paperback by Hodder Children's Books are natural recyclable
products made from wood grown in sustainable forests. The manufacturing processes
conform to the environmental regulations of the country of origin.

Hodder Children's Books
A division of Hodder Headline Ltd, 338 Euston Road, London NW1 3BH

CONTENTS

Coach Commotion
PAGE 7

Runaway Rollacoaster
PAGE 31

Star Surprise
PAGE 55

Coach Commotion

Felicity Wishes was renowned in Little Blossoming for her long lie-ins. It was usual to see Felicity dashing from her house late for school each morning.

But this morning Felicity woke even before her alarm went off!

For weeks now Felicity and her fairy friends had been counting down the days until today, and finally it had arrived. It was the day of the School of Nine Wishes annual outing

and the fairies were going to Sparkle Towers, the largest fairy theme park ever built.

"You're early!" said Polly in disbelief, as Felicity landed with an un-fairylike thud beside her. Holly, Polly and Daisy were in the school car park waiting for the coach to arrive. There were excited fairies everywhere, chattering and giggling.

"Phew!" said Felicity. "I flew as fast as I could. I couldn't risk missing the coach, not today!"

"Here already?" said Daisy, looking half-asleep. "That's not like you. Are you sure you haven't forgotten anything?"

"I packed my bag last night," said Felicity, rummaging around inside her bag. "Wand... pencil case... notebook... camera... keys... and... um... and..." Felicity's cheeks flushed as she rummaged a little deeper,

"… and most importantly…"

Holly and Daisy leaned forward expectantly.

"Sweets!" cried Felicity as she pulled out an enormous bag of strawberry fizzes, raspberry laces and blackberry sherbets. "You can't go on a school trip without sweets!"

Holly and Daisy cheered.

"What about your packed lunch?" asked Polly sensibly.

"Well," said Felicity, "I did think about that, but my packed lunch box wouldn't fit into this bag. And I had to bring this bag because it matches my outfit." Felicity loved to be the height of fashion at all times.

"But, Felicity, you can't eat sweets all day," exclaimed Polly. Polly desperately wanted to be a Tooth Fairy when she left the School of Nine Wishes and the importance of teeth hygiene was always at the forefront of her mind.

"Of course I can!" said Felicity. "I much prefer sweets to sandwiches anyway."

Polly couldn't believe what she was hearing. However, she didn't want to spoil the start of a magical day with a lecture so instead she made a mental note to send Felicity the latest leaflet on "Fairy Teeth". "Well, if you change your mind you can always share my sandwiches," she added.

The coach arrived and the class of excited fairies bundled on in a disorderly fashion.

"Quick!" said Holly, pushing her way to the front of the queue. "Let's grab the back seats!"

"Oh no! Someone's bags are on them already!" said Felicity, disappointed.

"They're my bags, silly!" said Daisy, popping up from behind one of the seats. "I was saving them for you three."

* * *

The four fairy friends spread out their things and made themselves comfortable on the back seat.

* * *

After Fairy Godmother had done a wand count, the coach started on its long journey to Sparkle Towers.

The trip had barely begun when Felicity, who had been too excited to eat breakfast, started feeling a little peckish.

"Sweet, anyone?" Felicity asked as she opened the enormous bag and waved it towards Holly, Polly and Daisy.

"At this time in the morning? No thanks," said Holly.

"I'm trying to give them up," said Polly. "You can't be a Tooth Fairy and eat sweets."

"Well, they're here if you change your mind," said Felicity, who happily began munching a strawberry fizz.

Suddenly the coach was filled with Fairy Godmother's voice.

"Testing, testing 1... 2... 3..." she said into a large microphone at the  front of the coach, tapping it twice with the end of her wand. "Welcome, fairies, to your annual school outing. As you know, the journey is a long one, so the teachers and I have come up with a short quiz to help pass the time. Miss Meandering will hand each of you a sheet with twenty questions. The person with the most correct answers will win a special mystery prize."

Felicity and her friends had already thought of how they'd like to pass the time on the journey, and it wouldn't leave much time for filling in a quiz!

Holly had brought her entire collection of *Fairy Girl* magazines, Polly had brought an electronic wand game to share, Daisy had brought her CD player and four sets of headphones, and Felicity had brought even more sweets!

Out of the window the scenery gradually changed as they left Little Blossoming, passed through Bloomfield, and meandered along country lanes. Most of the fairies had never been further than the outskirts of the town itself. They spent the first part of the journey with their noses pressed up against the windows in awe at the passing scenery.

Felicity and her friends whiled away the morning playing "Friendship Wave". Each fairy had to wave out of the back window at passing fairies and the fairy that got the most waves

back was the winner. Felicity won
every game because, being a very
friendly fairy, she waved at everyone.

"Are you sure you don't want a
sandwich, Felicity?" asked Polly,
tucking into her lunch. "I thought
strawberry jam sandwiches were your
favourite?"

"They are," said Felicity, unwrapping
another tube of sweets. "But I've got
plenty more sweets and they're much
yummier than jam sandwiches!"

The coach bumped along steadily and sunshine flooded in through the windows making drowsy fairies with full tummies fall into a deep sleep.

While the rest of the coach enjoyed its gentle slumber after lunch, Felicity's wings began to quiver, slowly at first but then at an uncontrollable and unstoppable speed!

"I don't feel so good," said Felicity, slowly handing back her copy of *Fairy Girl* to Holly.

"You look like you've got ants in your pants," said Polly, who had

opened one eye from her snooze to see what was making the seat jiggle.

"Can I have one of your sweets?" asked Daisy, pulling off her headphones.

"Have them all!" said Felicity, passing Daisy her bag. "I couldn't eat another sweet if I tried."

Daisy opened the bag and looked inside. "Felicity!" she squealed. "There's none left! You've eaten them all! That's why you feel sick!"

Felicity was now bouncing up and down so high on her seat that her crown kept touching the ceiling. "I can't sit still!" she said nervously.

"No wonder you've got so much energy, with all the additives in those sweets!" said Polly, eyeing up the content list on the back of one of the packs.

Just then Fairy Godmother's voice came through the loud speakers.

"Fairies, soon we will be stopping at a service station for petrol. It will be an ideal opportunity for you to stretch your wings for five minutes. If you do leave the coach, please return straight to your seats for a wand count before we set off."

Felicity couldn't wait to take full opportunity of the break to stretch her wings. Once outside, her friends watched in shock as Felicity flew frantically around and around, in any direction the wind  took her! Felicity had never flown so fast in her entire fairy life. When she finally landed with a crash beside her friends, her wings were still quivering.

"I'm never going to eat another

sweet ever again!" said
Felicity, out of breath. "I feel so
tired but I just can't stop moving!"

"I'm exhausted just watching you!"
said Holly.

"I hope you're going to have some
energy left to enjoy the theme park,"
said Polly, concerned.

"At least you'll have had a lot of
practice for the Big Dipper and the
Loop-the-loop!" said Daisy giggling.

✳ ✳ ✳

When all the fairies were back on the coach, Fairy Godmother began her wand count.

"Please raise your wands so I can make sure everyone is here," she boomed down the microphone. "And please try to keep still on the back row!" she added, as Felicity jiggled uncontrollably up and down on her seat.

As the coach set off for the second part of the journey, Holly, Polly, Daisy and Felicity looked at the mess they had made on the back seat.

There wasn't a magazine that hadn't been read or a CD that hadn't been listened to, the batteries of the electronic wand game had run out, and Felicity's sweet wrappers were all over the place! The fairies quickly tidied up their mess before Fairy Godmother made her way to the back of the coach.

"I'm bored!" said Holly, pressing her nose up against the window and pulling a face at a passing fairy.

"Let's do the quiz," said Polly. "It will help Felicity to keep her mind off her wings," she added. Polly rummaged around under the pile of *Fairy Girl* magazines and produced the quiz sheets Miss Meandering had given them earlier. "Has anyone got a pen?" she asked.

Daisy and Holly shrugged. Felicity felt down the side of her seat. 'I did have one," said Felicity as her arm slowly disappeared between the seats, "but I've lost it. I'll ask in front," she suggested.

Wings jiggling, Felicity knelt up on her seat and leant across to the seat in front. "Excuse me. Have you got a spare pen I can…" she said, stopping mid-sentence when she realised there was no one there. "Where's the fairy who was sitting in front of us?" said Felicity turning to her friends.

"The quiet one with bunches?" said Polly, who had noticed her when they got on the coach at school that morning. "I think she's called Rosie."

"I haven't seen her since we stopped at the service station," said Daisy thoughtfully. "She was in the queue behind me in the shop."

"Don't worry," said Holly. "We can borrow a pen from someone else."

But Felicity wasn't worried about the pen and was already bouncing down the aisle to see if she could find Rosie. By the time she reached Fairy Godmother at the front it was clear that Rosie wasn't on the coach.

"This is very serious," said Fairy Godmother when Felicity explained she thought they had left someone behind. "I had everyone present when I did the wand count... unless..." she said, watching Felicity jiggle up and down, "I counted someone's wand twice!"

Suddenly, Felicity stopped bouncing for the first time in hours and looked down at the floor. "I think I had a bad reaction to eating too many sweets," she said guiltily, starting to bounce again.

Fairy Godmother was thoughtful for a moment. "Stop the coach!" she ordered the driver. "There's only one thing for it," she explained to Felicity. "We shall have to abandon our trip to Sparkle Towers. There isn't enough time to drive all the way back to the service station, pick Rosie up, and come back again."

"Oh, it's all my fault!" said Felicity, feeling another surge of energy unsettle her wings. "Everyone will be so disappointed."

Fairy Godmother was just about to break the bad news to the rest of the fairies when Felicity had an idea that would put her excess wing power to good use.

"Fairy Godmother," she burst out, "I'll go and get her! My wings have been fluttering at four times their normal speed without me even trying. If you tell the driver to wait here, we'll be back before you can wave your wand!"

And before Fairy Godmother could stop her, Felicity had opened the coach door and was winging her way back to the service station.

* * *

As she neared the spot where they had stopped earlier, Felicity could see Rosie sitting alone on the steps in front of the shop. When Felicity landed in front of her, Rosie looked up and beamed the biggest smile Felicity had ever seen.

"Oh, I'm so pleased to see you! I couldn't decide which magazine to buy and when I came out of the shop the coach had gone! I've been looking forward to this trip to Sparkle Towers all year. I can't bear to think I've missed it," she said, hugging Felicity tightly.

"You haven't missed it yet!" said Felicity, feeling another wing rush. "Hold tightly on to my wand. I'm going to fly you back to join the others faster than any fairground ride!"

And with that they were off!

Felicity and Rosie flew at top speed over countryside and towns, up into the hills and down into valleys, until they reached the coach of anxious fairies.

A loud cheer erupted as Felicity and Rosie climbed the steps to board the coach. Now everyone would be able to enjoy plenty of time at Sparkle Towers.

"Hip, Hip, Hooray!" the fairies chorused.

As the coach set off again to continue its journey, Fairy Godmother

spoke into the microphone once more.

"When you have all settled down you might like to find your quiz sheets and quietly check you have answered all your questions before Miss Meandering comes round to collect them. The mystery prize will be given on arrival at Sparkle Towers."

As Felicity headed back towards her seat, Fairy Godmother quietly stopped her. "I'm afraid I can't allow you to enter the quiz any more, Felicity," she said solemnly.

"I understand," said Felicity, a little upset. "I did cause a lot of a bother."

"Well, that's not the reason you can't enter," said Fairy Godmother cryptically. "You see," and she bent forward to whisper into Felicity's ear, "the mystery prize for the quiz is a gigantic bag of sweets!"

The least expected
advantages

come from the
most unexpected
places

Runaway Rollacoaster

"Wow!" said Felicity Wishes, looking up, open-mouthed, at the glittering golden gateway to Sparkle Towers. "It's beautiful!" Excited fairies from the School of Nine Wishes chattered all around her.

"I've never been to a fairground before," said Daisy excitedly.

"I don't think any of us have been to a fairground like this before," commented Fairy Godmother, and turning to the fairies, she continued, "Sparkle Towers is the largest fairground in the whole of Fairy World.

If you look to your left you will see the famous Flutter Wheel. Completed only last year, it has entered the Fairy Book of Records as the tallest fairground wheel ever to be made, and boasts views from the top of exceptional beauty."

Fairy Godmother waved them in and, with a flutter of excited fairy wings, the fairies flew single file through the gates.

"Don't forget," called Fairy Godmother after them, "be back at the coach before it gets dark. Have fun!"

"This is going to be the best school trip ever!" said Polly, flying high above the ground, trying to catch a glimpse of the famous Flutter Wheel.

Felicity, Holly, Daisy, and Polly didn't know where to start. Every direction they glanced towards held glittering treats and amazing rides.

Twinkly fairground music filled their ears while their eyes darted from candy floss stalls to beautifully coloured merry-go-rounds, from dodgem cars to big dippers, and from ice-cream treats to magic mirrors. There were smiling fairy faces everywhere.

"What shall we go on first?" said Holly, eagerly jiggling up and down on the spot.

"It has to be the Flutter Wheel!" said Polly, who had been dreaming about the view from the top ever since the school trip had been announced.

"Come on then!" said Felicity, waving her fairground map. "Follow me!" she said confidently, although the other fairies knew Felicity was hopeless at reading maps.

By the time they had made two detours, stopped to read the map three times, and then stopped to ask the way, there was long queue of fairies waiting for their turn on the Flutter Wheel.

"Oh no!" said Felicity, looking at the two hour waiting sign.

"What shall we do now?" said Holly, a little annoyed that it had taken them so long to reach the ride.

"I think we should save the best ride until last!" said Polly, trying to keep everyone jolly.

"I'm sure the queue will be much shorter later on," agreed Daisy. "What about the log flume? Let's go on that!"

Holly looked unimpressed. "It looks very wet," she said, swishing her perfectly groomed locks. "It could ruin the hours of hard work I spent blow-drying my hair this morning."

"Log flumes are supposed to be wet, silly!" said Polly. "Perhaps you could go for the 'tousled' look today?" she said giggling.

Felicity, Polly and Daisy wouldn't take no for an answer and dragged Holly to the ride.

"Oh, OK then," she mumbled. "But if my hair gets wet then you will all have to treat me to a makeover at Fairy Hair."

✳ ✳ ✳

Felicity and her friends were so busy giggling at the soggy fairies stumbling off the ride that their turn came quicker than they expected.

As the attendant lifted the rope for them to move on to the boarding platform, Felicity suddenly saw a fairy giving out hats in the crowd.

"I'm just popping to get something," she said quietly to Daisy. "I'll be back in a second."

When she returned, her friends were nowhere to be seen.

"Over here!" called Holly waving from the log boat, which was slowly moving away from the platform. "Sorry, we tried to wait for you, but the attendant said that she couldn't hold things up. Where did you go?"

"I went to get you this!" said Felicity, throwing a waterproof hat over the barrier to land right on Holly's head!

"Thanks, Felicity!" shouted Holly as the log boat made its way to the top of a huge gushing waterfall.

Holly hid behind Daisy and Daisy squeezed Polly's hand tightly. "I'm not sure I want to do this," said Daisy, her voice wobbling as she looked down at the big drop.

"Too late nowwwwwwwwwwwww," cried Polly as the log was released and shot down the chute with a

thunderous roar,
spraying gallons of
water everywhere.
"Ahhhhhhhhhhhh!"
they all squealed
at once. Holly
held on to
her hat with
both hands,
Daisy wrapped her
wings tightly around herself, and
Polly, who had decided that she might
as well just go for it, flung both her
arms above her head!

With the most enormous SPLASH,
the log boat crashed into the pool at
the bottom, soaking them all from
head to toe.

Three dripping fairies made their
way to the exit, where Felicity was
waiting. "I hear the wet look is all
the rage this season," said Felicity
in fits of giggles.

Holly skipped up to
Felicity and gave her
a big soggy hug.
"Thanks for my hat,
Felicity," she said,
realising that the
only part of her that
wasn't wet was her hair!

"That was an amazing ride," said
Daisy.

"Incredible! It's such a shame you
missed it, Felicity," said Polly.

"I think I had just as much fun
watching you!" said Felicity, still
giggling.

✳ ✳ ✳

The warm golden sunshine was soon
drying their wings as they headed off
to the next ride.

"Felicity, you should choose what
we go on next because you missed out
on the fun of the first ride," said Polly.

"What about the carousel?"

suggested Felicity. "It's my favourite ride and your dresses can dry in the wind as we go round!"

Daisy clapped her hands "What a lovely idea!" she said.

As the excited fairies approached the ride, Felicity saw something that would make the ride even lovelier for her friends.

"You three jump on, I'm just going to get something! Save the pink horse for me!" she said, skipping off in the opposite direction.

Daisy, Holly and Polly gracefully fluttered onto the backs of three beautifully painted wooden horses. Polly closed her eyes and let the wind billow through her hair. She

was just thinking to herself that
things couldn't be more perfect when
Felicity interrupted her thoughts.

"Strawberry, banana, chocolate or
raspberry?" she asked, holding four
enormous ice-creams.

"Ooh, lovely!" said Polly as she
reached for the banana ice-cream.
"You're full of great ideas today,
Felicity!"

Felicity passed round the rest
of the cones and settled on the
back of the pink horse with her
favourite strawberry ice-cream.
She was just about to take a
big lick when Polly cried out.

"I feel dizzy! I'm not very good
on rides that go round and round,"
she said with a wobbling voice.

The attendant looked up. "You
should probably sit down and have a
rest," she suggested.

Felicity knew how horrible it was to

feel ill, so she offered to keep Polly
company until she felt better. "I'm not
having much luck with rides today,"
she thought, trying not to feel sorry
for herself. Slowly she took out the
fairground map from her pocket and
unfolded it.

＊ ＊ ＊

"Look," said Polly, pointing to the
corner of the map. "A ghost train!
Let's go on that next!"

Daisy looked
uncertain. "You
go on without
me," she said.

"Come on, it
will be fun!" said
Holly. "It's only
a ride."

"It's just that it's such a beautiful
day I don't want to sit in the dark,"
Daisy replied quietly.

Felicity knew Daisy was afraid of

the dark so she shuffled next to her and whispered softly into her ear, "You can sit next to me if you like and hold my hand if you get scared."

Daisy smiled at Felicity. "Although, on second thoughts, it does look like it might rain. Maybe I will come after all," she said to the other fairies.

When the fairies reached the ride it looked closed.

"Where is everyone?" asked Holly suspiciously.

The ghost ride looked ancient. A rickety old train covered in cobwebs with four empty carriages. There wasn't even an attendant.

The four fairy friends boarded the battered train.

"Isn't this a treat?" said Felicity. "No queue, and the whole ride to ourselves. If only the Flutter Wheel was like this!"

"We must make the Flutter Wheel

our next ride before the fairground closes. We don't want to miss the main attraction," said Polly.

Without warning, the train pulled off with a sharp jolt, making Daisy's wings quiver even more. It creaked and shook as it slowly headed towards two huge black doors draped with crawling ivy. As they neared the doors, Felicity could see they were covered with spiders too!

"They are only pretend, I'm sure," she said, grabbing Daisy's hand and squeezing it tightly.

Daisy wasn't remotely scared of spiders – she wanted to be a Blossom Fairy when she graduated from the School of Nine Wishes and was used to seeing spiders in her garden – but she knew that Felicity was terrified of creepy-crawlies, so she squeezed her hand back.

With a loud clap the doors flew

open, making Holly and Polly jump
so far out of their seats that they
landed in each other's seats!

"I'm not sure this was such a good
idea," said Polly nervously.

The train had entered a room that
was completely black.

"I can't see a thing," said Holly,
panicking.

* * *

Very slowly the train squeaked eerily
along the track.

"Are we still moving?" asked Felicity,
feeling a cold shiver run down her
back.

"I think so," whispered Daisy. She might not have been scared of spiders but the blackness made her feel very uncertain indeed.

As their eyes grew more accustomed to the dark, the fairies could just about make out cobwebs and slimy green goo that hung from the ceiling and walls.

"Arghhhh!" squealed Holly. "Something just brushed past my face."

Suddenly, there was a low, deep moan. "OOOOOOOooooooooo."

"Daisy, it's OK. Don't be scared," said Felicity firmly, even though she was struggling to stop her own wings from trembling. "I'm here."

"That wasn't *me* moaning!" said Daisy in the darkness.

"It wasn't me or Polly either!" said Holly.

The fairies fell silent.

"OOOOOOOOOOoooooooooooo," came the noise again.

"Aaahhhhhhhhhhhhh!" screamed the fairies together.

"It's just a fairground ride, remember," said Felicity, trying to calm everyone down as well as herself.

As the train crawled along the track, they heard the moan again. "OOOOOooooooooo." This time it was louder. The fairies' wings pricked up in fright!

Without warning, the carriage came to a sharp halt and all four fairies lurched forward in their seats.

"Let's get out of here!" said Holly, scrambling off the train.

"We'll never find the way out in the dark," said Polly frantically.

Then they heard a distinctly un-monster-type voice. "Where are yoOOOOOOOOOoooooooo?

There you are! At last!"

The fairies turned to see a very tall fairy with long hair walking towards them with a torch.

"I'm glad I finally found you," the fairy said. "The ghost train is closed for refurbishment. You must have missed the notice at the entrance. Let me introduce myself: I'm Wanda Sparkle, the owner of Sparkle Towers."

Neither Holly, Polly, Daisy or Felicity could speak.

"It looks as though I've given you all rather a big shock," said Wanda, concerned. She looked at her watch. "Unfortunately all the rides have taken their last trip but, if you come back tomorrow, I'll arrange for you to ride on any attraction you choose without queuing."

Felicity finally found her voice. "That's very kind of you," she explained, "but we're on a school day trip."

Polly's wings drooped and Felicity knew why. She'd been looking forward to riding the Flutter Wheel too. "Perhaps we will be lucky enough to come again next year and ride your famous Flutter Wheel," she said, trying to look on the bright side.

"You haven't been on the Flutter Wheel?" said Wanda, shocked. "Well, in that case I shall do something very special. Follow me!"

Wanda Sparkle led the fairies to the base of the Flutter Wheel and handed them four glittering golden tickets. "Please accept these exclusive passes as an apology for having such a dreadful ride on our ghost train. I'll let your party leader know that you'll be a bit late. Enjoy the ride!"

Felicity and her friends boarded the ride as fast as they could before anything else could go wrong. Inside the beautiful glass carriage were four golden chairs padded with luxurious cherry red velvet. As they sat down, the doors silently closed and the wheel began to turn the carriage high into the sky and way above the clouds.

When they reached the top the view was more amazing than any of them had imagined. The sun was setting and Sparkle Towers was aglow with the most beautiful shades of pink.

"I never knew pink could look so beautiful," said Felicity, totally in awe. But the other fairies were too busy admiring the stunning view to answer her.

frightening things
are less scary

with friends

Star Surprise

Felicity Wishes wriggled restlessly on the back seat of the coach. It had been a long day but the School of Nine Wishes annual outing was now over and they were heading home.

"I'm bored!" sighed Holly, looking out of the window.

"Me too," said Daisy, putting down the latest edition of *Fairy Girl* magazine. "I've read this copy from cover to cover."

"I know, let's play I Spy!" suggested Felicity. She loved playing games with her friends.

Daisy, who had been trying to get to sleep for ages, reluctantly opened one eye.

"I'll play too. It's impossible to get to sleep sitting up. I've got pins and needles in my wings!"

"Good idea!" said Felicity. "Daisy, you go first."

"I spy with my little eye, something beginning with..." and Daisy scoured the coach for inspiration. "Something beginning with..." and she stared out of the window. "Something beginning with... oh goodness!"

"Beginning with 'oh goodness'?" said Felicity giggling. "That's not a letter. You're supposed to begin I Spy with a single letter of the alphabet!"

"I know!" said Daisy, "But look!" and she pointed out of the coach window.

"OH GOODNESS," all four fairy friends chorused.

Standing tall against the passing hedgerow and gradually disappearing into the distance was a large signpost pointing to Little Blossoming in the opposite direction!

"Oh no! We're going the wrong way!" said Felicity, trying not to panic.

"The driver must be lost!" said Polly, feeling a little uneasy.

"We must tell Fairy Godmother!" said Felicity. "Or we'll never get home."

"What if we run out of petrol and have to spend the night in the coach?" squealed Holly. "It is essential that I get my beauty sleep."

Holly was the most dramatic of all the fairy friends and enjoyed turning even the most normal situations into a crisis.

Felicity stood up and wobbled as quietly as she could down the aisle so as not to wake up her sleeping classmates.

When she got to the front she found Fairy Godmother and Miss Meandering both fast asleep.

Felicity coughed a little louder than she'd intended.

Miss Meandering woke up with such a start that she almost lost her crown! As she scrambled to catch it, a large brown envelope slid off the teacher's lap and on to the floor.

Felicity bent down to pick it up. The writing on the front caught her eye; it read "Rock Tickets". Felicity smiled to herself at her teacher's obsession with all things geological.

"Sorry to wake you both," whispered Felicity quietly. "Only I have something very important to tell you. I think the driver's lost. We're going in the wrong direction!"

"What time is it?" asked Fairy Godmother more calmly than Felicity expected.

"It's seven o'clock," replied Felicity, glancing at the coach clock.

"Is it that time already?" Fairy Godmother gasped, quickly standing up. "I have something very important to tell you all."

Fairy Godmother picked up the microphone and stood to face the sleeping fairies. "Wakey, wakey, fairies!" she boomed down the microphone.

"Sorry to wake you from your dreams but I have a magical mystery surprise for you! We've been invited to see a very special display."

The coachload of fairies looked puzzled.

Fairy Godmother continued, "In precisely ten minutes we will arrive at our destination. Have your coats on ready, and, most importantly, don't forget your cameras. It certainly promises to be a very entertaining evening."

The sleepy coachful of fairies suddenly erupted into an excited giggling mass of fluttering wings.

Holly, Polly and Daisy already had their coats on and their cameras on their laps by the time Felicity had made it back to her seat. They were beaming with expectant smiles and speculating about the magical mystery surprise.

"I hope it's
a visit to the
Midnight Gardens,"
said Daisy, "I've read
that the rare flowers
only come out at night
in the most luminous
colours you could
ever imagine."

"I bet it's a trip
to see Stella
Fluttiano's latest fashion show," said
Holly. "Although I hear they only
allow the most fashionable fairies to
attend," she said, swishing her hair
dramatically.

"I suppose it would be too much
to expect it to be a visit to see
'Toothpaste Through the Ages' at the
Fairy Science Museum?" asked Polly,
who longed to be a Tooth Fairy.

Felicity looked at Holly and Daisy
in horror! Even Miss Meandering's

rock lecture would be livelier than that, thought Felicity.

Felicity didn't want to ruin her friends' excitement but, at the same time, she couldn't bear to see their disappointment when they discovered what Fairy Godmother had in store for them. She took a deep breath and addressed them solemnly.

"I know I really shouldn't be telling you this but..." she paused, looking at her friends' eager faces, "... the magical mystery surprise is a geology lecture on rocks. I've just seen an envelope with the tickets inside."

Holly, Polly and Daisy's wings drooped.

"No midnight flowers?" asked Daisy.

"No hot new looks?" asked Holly.

"No history of toothpaste?" asked Polly.

"Nope, just boring rocks!" said

Felicity, feeling just as disappointed as her friends.

* * *

The coach pulled up outside a large arena and, in single file, the coachload of excited fairies flew through the turnstiles and found their seats. Felicity and her friends followed at a slow pace.

Hundreds of fairies sat tier upon tier in the circular arena. Brightly coloured lights lit a magnificent stage and huge sound speakers stood all around.

"How in fairy world are we going to see rock samples from here?" said Holly, looking down at the stage, which appeared tiny from where they were sitting.

"Look," said Polly, pointing with her pen, "there's an enormous screen just above the main stage. They'll show them on there."

Polly was the most studious of all the fairy friends and was actually looking forward to taking notes on all the different types of rock that made up Fairy World.

Suddenly the lights dimmed and the whole arena was in darkness. A few excited squeals erupted randomly into the silence as everyone waited.

"I never thought rocks were so popular," whispered Holly to Felicity, and just then the speakers blasted out the opening bars of some music they all recognised. It was the first song on their favourite album by the world famous Suzi Sparkle.

"What an odd song to choose for the opening of a lecture on rocks," said Felicity to her friends.

All of a sudden, lights of every colour of the rainbow flooded the stage. The music boomed louder and louder. Fairies all around were screaming with excitement. Then the lights dimmed and on to the stage walked...
SUZI SPARKLE!

Felicity, Holly, Polly and Daisy jumped up and screamed along with the rest of the audience. Suzi Sparkle was the most famous fairy rock star in the whole of Fairy World. Felicity and her friends had spent hours learning the songs, copying her dance routines, and pretending they were backing singers for Suzi Sparkle. But they never dreamed that, one day, they would see their greatest idol performing at a live rock concert!

"I don't believe it!" screamed Holly above the music.

"Neither do I!" said Felicity, delighted that she had been so wrong about the rock lecture.

It was the best mystery magical surprise ever. Felicity could barely wait to go and thank Fairy Godmother at half-time for organising such a wonderful treat. Tickets to see Suzi Sparkle were like gold dust!

* * *

Every single fairy in the arena knew all the words to Suzi's songs, but it was Felicity and her three friends that knew the moves to her dance routines as well. By the time Suzi had come to the end of the first half of the show, Felicity, Holly, Polly and Daisy were pooped!

"That was SPARKLETASTIC!" screamed Daisy, forgetting that she no longer needed to shout above the music.

"I'm going to get some water," said

Felicity. "Does anyone want me to bring anything back?"

"Nope," said Polly, slumped in her seat. "I'm going to rest here and get my energy back for the second half."

* * *

Felicity became quite hot and bothered as she squeezed her way through the large crowd of fairies queuing for a drink. Seeing a passage away from the crowds, Felicity decided to slip down it and rest in the quiet for a few moments.

She wandered along the passage for a while, looking for a less crowded drinks stall. She finally came across a water cooler and poured herself a large glass.

As she sipped her icy drink, she heard the music over the tannoy and started to practise a dance routine she had made up in her bedroom the previous night. Felicity twirled to the left, fluttered to the right and pirouetted down the corridor without a care in the world.

Suddenly, Felicity was aware that she was not alone. In the shadows of the passage, another fairy was watching her every move.

"Hot, isn't it?" said Felicity panting, and slightly embarrassed that she hadn't noticed the fairy earlier. "Would you like some water? It's lovely and cool!"

"I'd love some," said the other fairy walking towards her. "It's even hotter on stage, you know. I just had to get away somewhere cool and quiet for a while."

As the fairy approached, Felicity couldn't quite believe her eyes. "Suzi Sparkle!" she gasped. Suzi was just as beautiful in real life, but much smaller than Felicity had imagined. Felicity busied herself with pouring a drink of water for Suzi, trying to hide her blushing cheeks.

"Thanks," said Suzi as Felicity passed the cup over.

"It's a great show," said Felicity, not daring to look at Suzi. "Your dance routines are magical!"

"Thank you," said Suzi, flattered. "To be honest I'm getting a little bored of doing the same old routines every time," she sighed. "You look like you had some great ideas just now."

"Loads!" said Felicity, whose favourite thing in the world, next to making friends, was dancing. Felicity felt her confidence come back as she showed Suzi some of her dazzling moves.

Time flew by and Felicity had only just finished showing Suzi her extra special "double loop shuffle step" when they heard the bell sound for everyone to return to their seats.

"I'd better get back to my seat," said Felicity, still glowing with

excitement. "I don't want to miss a second of your show!"

"Thanks," said Suzi, giving her a hug. "I feel inspired again!"

Bbbrrrrrinnnnng

"That's the last bell, you'd better fly," said Suzi. "I've just thought," she continued as Felicity turned to go, "I don't know what your name is."

"Felicity," called Felicity as she flew towards the door of the arena, "Felicity Wishes."

Felicity flew back to her seat as fast as her wings could take her, desperate to tell her friends all about meeting Suzi Sparkle.

"You were a long time," whispered Holly across the row to Felicity.

"You'll never believe this, but I've just been teaching Suzi Sparkle new dance routines," replied Felicity.

Holly, Polly and Daisy looked at
her in disbelief "Ha ha," said Polly,
assuming that Felicity was joking.

"No, really," said Felicity. "I really
was. She was so nice and so normal.
Just like one of us."

"Yeah, right," said Holly, raising
her eyebrows. "Just like it was true
that we were coming to see a geology
lecture and not a rock concert."

"Oh," said Felicity, a little hurt that
her friends didn't believe her. "That
was just a simple mistake."

Before Felicity had time to convince

her friends she was telling the truth,
the lights went down and Suzi
Sparkle was back on stage.

* * *

The second half of the concert was
just as good as the first. All four fairy
friends had almost lost their voices
and danced their tights off by the
time the final encore came.

"For my last song, I'm going to try
something new," shouted Suzi into

the microphone, struggling to make herself heard above the cries for more. "This is a favourite song of mine that you all know..." the crowd cheered louder than ever, "... but, just for tonight, I'm going to put it to a sparkling new dance routine that I couldn't have learnt without the help of my new friend, Felicity Wishes! This one's for you, Felicity!"

Suzi waved into the audience at Felicity.

Holly, Polly and Daisy stared open-mouthed at Felicity as she waved wildly back at Suzi.

"I'll teach you all the steps later," she shouted above the music, giggling at her friends' stunned faces.

* * *

It was a magical end to a magical day.

If you enjoyed this book, why not try another of these fantastic story collections?

Clutter Clean-out

Designer Drama

Newspaper Nerves

Star Surprise

Also available in the Felicity Wishes range:

Felicity Wishes: Snowflakes and Sparkledust

It is time for spring to arrive in Little Blossoming but there is a problem and winter is staying put. Can Felicity Wishes get the seasons back on track?

Felicity Wishes: Secrets and Surprises

Felicity Wishes is planning her birthday party but it seems none of her friends can come. Will Felicity end up celebrating her birthday alone?

Felicity Wishes has lots to say in these fantastic little books:

Little Book of Love

Little Book of Peace

Little Book of Hiccups

Little Book of Every Day Wishes

Little Book of Fun